WILD SURPRISE

Adapted by Helena Mayer

Based on the series created by Dan Povenmire & Jeff "Swampy" Marsh

DISNEP PRESS

New York

Printed in the United States of America
3 5 7 9 10 6 8 4 2

Library of Congress Catalog Card Number on file.
ISBN 978-1-4231-1798-8

For more Disney Press fun, visit www.disneybooks.com.
Visit DisneyChannel.com

Part One

Chapter 1

Phineas Flynn popped up in bed, his eyes wide open.

"Hey, Ferb!" Phineas tossed a pillow across the room, aiming for his brother, who was still fast asleep. Phineas didn't get it. How could Ferb sleep on a day like this?

After all, it wasn't just any day.

This was *it*, the *big* day. The day Phineas had been waiting for all summer long. "It's

Candace's birthday!" he shouted, blasting Ferb out of dreamland. "We *gotta* do better than last year."

Last year's birthday had started out okay. Candace had loved her cake. It was chocolate chocolate chip (her favorite) and covered in pink-and-white frosting (her double favorite).

But it never occurred to Phineas that Candace was afraid of gorillas.

Especially giant gorillas hiding inside birthday cakes.

"Not our best work,"

Phineas admitted. Ferb didn't say anything, but Phineas could tell he agreed. "This time, it's gotta be something huge!"

This year, Phineas was determined to give his sister a birthday present that wouldn't make her scream and run out of the room. And he knew just how to do it.

This is the greatest birthday ever, Candace thought, settling back into her giant, gold birthday throne. A handsome man in a tuxedo stood on a stage shaped like a birthday cake. He sang a song written just for her.

"She's Candace," he crooned. "Candace! Candace! Like the Venus de Milo. Except she's not armless and handless. She's got a big honkin' truckload of ship-launching qualities, and this is the reason she bears no resemblance to a praying mantis."

Backup singers swarmed around Candace, handing her a bouquet of flowers and a heavy, golden birthday crown.

"Candace!" they sang in harmony. "A name with seven letters.

"Candace! Only wears designer sweaters.

"Candace! She's got an allergy to dairy.

"Candace! That chick's anything but ordinary!"

It was everything she could have wanted in a birthday: music, cake, spotlights, dancing, Perry the Platypus—Perry the Platypus?!?

It was all a dream. Candace scowled. Do I get a birthday wish? she thought sourly. Because I wish I were still asleep.

Chapter 2

Candace scooped up Perry and stormed down to the kitchen. She plopped the platypus into Phineas's lap. "This is yours, I believe," she snapped.

"Happy birthday, Candace!" her mom trilled, carrying a plate of pancakes over toward the table. "I made you a special breakfast!"

Ooh, pancakes! Candace thought. And not just pancakes. Extraspecial *birthday* pancakes, with a candle on top. Linda Flynn-Fletcher wasn't the best cook, but she made *excellent* birthday pancakes. Candace brightened. Maybe this wouldn't be such a putrid birthday after all.

"And after that, we have a surprise," Candace's stepfather said, looking up from his bowl of oatmeal. Lawrence Fletcher was originally from England, and his British accent made a birthday surprise sound even better.

"What is it?" Candace gasped. She *loved* surprises. Especially birthday surprises.

(Unless they involved gorillas.) "What is it?"

"We have to drive to it," her dad said.

"Ooh!" she clasped her hands together, trying not to squeal. If they were driving to her surprise, that meant it *had* to be good.

Right?

After breakfast, the whole family piled into the car.

Candace asked her mother where they were going. But Linda wouldn't say.

So she asked her step-dad.

No luck.

She even asked Phineas and Ferb, but they kept their mouths shut.

The car sped down the road. Wherever they were going, it was taking forever.

"Is it the mall?" she guessed. Please let it be the mall, she thought. That would be the best birthday surprise ever. The mall. The mall. The mall.

"No," her mom said.

"Okay." Candace sighed. But then she had an idea: maybe fooling her was just part of the surprise. "But it's the mall, right?" she asked hopefully.

"No, it's not the mall," Lawrence said firmly.

A moment later, he turned the car off the main road. They sped past a sign for Mount Rushmore.

"Wait," Candace said. She was starting to get a bad feeling. The kind of feeling you get when your family drags you to a totally boring national monument and tries to pretend it's a

fun birthday surprise. "Please don't tell me we're going to Mount Rushmore!"

Linda twisted around to smile at her from the front seat. "Isn't it great?" she gushed. "Four American presidents, carved into the side of a *mountain*."

"It was Phineas and Ferb's idea!" her stepdad added.

Candace sighed. Of course it was.

Candace's dad pulled up in front of the main entrance. "Okay, you lot go on ahead," he said. "I'll find a parking spot and meet you there."

"We're going up to the monument," Phineas announced as his stepdad drove away. He tugged at Ferb. "Come on, Perry." Obedient as ever, the pet platypus lumbered after them, toward the mountain.

"Okay, we'll join you in a minute," Linda called, waving good-bye to the boys. Then she led Candace straight for the gift shop. Candace gaped at the tables and shelves stuffed full of ugly Mount Rushmore souvenirs. "Okay, Candace, it's your birthday. You can pick out anything you want."

"Ooh!" Her mom snatched up a plastic model of the monument. Four presidents'

heads wobbled on metal springs. "What about the Mount Rushmore bobble heads?"

Candace rolled her eyes. In a store full of ugly, the bobble-head toys took the prize. Candace thought it might even have broken a world record for ugliness. "Mom, that's lame!"

Her mother moved on to an ugly stuffed president. "Okay, how about this cute Cuddle-Me Lincoln?"

Candace decided it was time to explain to her mother the meaning of the word *lame*. And the

fact that if you looked up *lame* in the dictionary, you'd probably find a picture of Cuddle-Me-Lincoln.

But before she could speak, Candace got distracted by something much more important than her mother's taste in souvenirs. She spotted a Mr. Slushy Burger sign hanging on the other side of the gift shop—and then she spotted a cute blond boy standing beneath it. A very *familiar* cute blond boy, looking even cuter than usual in his Mr. Slushy Burger uniform.

"Jeremy?" she squawked.

Get it together, she told herself. You sound like a chicken.

Candace batted her eyes. Stay calm, she thought. Cool and casual, that's me. "Hi, Jeremy!" she said brightly as she bounced on her toes a little.

Jeremy grinned. Candace really liked his grin.

Could he hear her heart pounding in her chest?

"Hey, Candace," he said.

She liked his voice about twenty times more than his grin!

Candace tried to talk, but nothing came out. Ugh! Why was it so hard to think of something to say? Maybe because her brain was overloaded by the realization that she was *actually* talking to Jeremy!

Or at least trying to talk to him.

CALM DOWN! she warned herself, rather uncalmly.

"What are you doing here?" she asked Jeremy, managing not to hyperventilate. Barely.

"I'm just here on the Mr. Slushy Burger worker-exchange program," he said.

"Um . . ." Candace forgot what she was going to say next. She glanced behind her at a huge window. She noticed she could see Phineas and Ferb heading for the mountain—and carrying rock-climbing equipment. They were definitely up to something. But *what?* Candace fumed.

Jeremy cleared his throat.

Oh. Right. *Jeremy.*

"Oh, well, it's my birthday today," she told him, "and I, uh—" Phineas and Ferb walked past the window again. This time, they were lugging jackhammers and pickaxes.

What were they *doing*?

Candace couldn't stand it anymore. She had to know.

Now.

"I gotta check something," she told Jeremy. "Back in a flash, 'kay?"

She was gone before he could answer.

Chapter 3

Phineas and Ferb were gone by the time Candace made it outside. They had places to go, mountains to climb. They were on a mission.

It wasn't until he was dangling off the side of Mount Rushmore that Phineas realized someone was missing. "Hey, where's Perry?"

Perry was on a mission of his own.

Or rather, *Agent P* was on a mission.

Most of the time, Perry the Platypus went where Phineas told him to go. He ate when Phineas told him to eat. He slept when Phineas told him to sleep. He made funny noises and performed funny tricks and, every once in a while, produced funny smells.

In other words, he acted like an ordinary pet platypus.

Most of the time.

But Perry *wasn't* an ordinary pet platypus. He was a secret agent, sworn to protect the world from evil. That's all evil, in general.

But Perry the Platypus spent most of his time battling a very specific evil. A brilliant, demented, out-of-his-mind evil named Dr. Doofenshmirtz. And while he was lumbering after Phineas and Ferb, Perry had received a secret message from his boss, Major

Monogram. Dr. Doofenshmirtz was about to strike again. And only Agent P could stop him.

That meant it was time to ditch his cover as the mild-mannered pet platypus. It also meant getting back to his home base, ASAP.

A secret passageway was hidden in one of the Mount Rushmore trash cans. As soon as Phineas's back was turned, Perry activated the trapdoor and dove inside. He dropped into a network of underground tubes and whooshed toward his base. It was filled with high-tech equipment, and computer 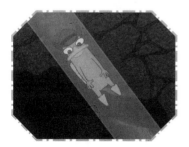 screens were broadcasting constant streams of data from all over the world. But Perry ignored them all, except for the large screen hanging in the

19

middle of the room.
He flicked it on.
Major Monogram's
face beamed down at him.

"Good morning, Agent P," the major boomed, glad to see his best operative was ready to go. "Dr. Doofenshmirtz is up to no good again. We've just discovered his new hideout is located inside Lincoln's head at Mount Rushmore."

Mount Rushmore?

Agent P narrowed his eyes at his boss. The major squirmed. "I . . . I know, you were just

there," he admitted, a little embarrassed. "Poor planning on our part, actually. Sorry."

Sorry didn't change the fact that Agent P now had to run out of his secret base, dive back into the system of underground tubes, and make it back to Mount Rushmore—all before Dr. Doofenshmirtz could complete his evil plan!

Would he make it in time?

As soon as he arrived back at the monument, Agent P retrieved the platypus-sized digging machine that Major Monogram had left for him. He positioned it on the top of George Washington's head, then began to drill through the aged granite. Soon he was on his way down to the center of Mount Rushmore.

The digging machine looked like an old tire with

a bunch of tiny drills taped on—but it was effective. Soon Perry reached a giant hollow in the heart of the mountain. He dismounted the digging machine and took a deep breath. The air stank of dirt and evil. Perry knew this was it: the newest hidden lair of Dr. Doofenshmirtz.

"Ah, Perry the Platypus," the mad scientist cackled, emerging from the depths of the cave. "Your timing is impeccable. And by 'impeccable,' I mean *completely peccable!*" He pressed a button on his remote control, and a thick glass wall dropped down between him and his nemesis. Perry banged against the glass with his fists, but it was no use. Dr. Doofenshmirtz was beyond his reach.

For now.

"You are just in time to witness my latest scheme." Dr. Doofenshmirtz stepped to the side, revealing a large vehicle. It looked like a rather odd-shaped truck with a sharp silver drill jutting out of its bumper. "Behold, my Drill-a-nator! I will bore a tunnel to China,

build a toll highway, and make millions." The evil scientist laughed an evil laugh. "So, as they say in China, *arrivederci*."

Perry pounded against the thick glass as Dr. Doofenshmirtz jumped into his Drill-a-nator. There was a thundering roar and, slowly but surely, the machine began tunneling through the floor of the hideaway and toward the center of the earth. Soon Dr. Doofenshmirtz was gone, and there was nothing Agent P could do to stop him.

Or was there?

Chapter 4

Candace didn't notice Perry the Platypus disappear into the trash can, and she didn't notice him popping out again. She *definitely* didn't notice him landing on top of Mount Rushmore and then drilling a tunnel into it. She was too busy searching for her brothers. But they were nowhere in sight.

Candace stood at the edge of the observation platform that overlooked the mountain.

Phineas and Ferb had to be *somewhere*, but where?

That's when she spotted the telescope. "Let me see that!" she cried, shoving the tourists out of the way.

Candace pressed her face to the lens and gasped. Phineas and Ferb were climbing up Abraham Lincoln's giant nose! It might have

been the craziest thing her brothers had ever done. And this time, there was no way they'd weasel out of getting caught.

Candace would make sure of it.

"Mom!" she shrieked. "Mom, you've got to see this *now!*"

Linda took an incredibly long time climbing up the steps to the observation platform. Candace hopped up and down, waiting and waiting . . . and waiting. Any minute now, Phineas and Ferb were going to get caught, once and for all. It would be the best birthday present, ever.

Finally, her mother made it to the top of the stairs and joined Candace at the telescope. "Here," Candace said, squashing her mother's face against eyepiece. "*Look!*"

But at this particular telescope, one quarter paid for five minutes of viewing time—and the five minutes were up. All Linda saw was black screen, with a single word written across it: EXPIRED.

"Oops," she said. "Ran out of time."

Frantic, Candace dug in her pocket for

another coin. She dropped it into the telescope. "Here, look now!"

Her mother peered through the eyepiece. But she didn't see Phineas and Ferb on the mountain.

She didn't even see the mountain.

All she saw was a gush of water, as the park's famous geyser spewed into the air, blocking the view of Mount Rushmore. "Oh, it's Old Reliable geyser. How exciting!" Linda exclaimed. She backed away from the telescope. "I'm just gonna go back to the gift shop."

There was nothing Candace could do to stop her.

Hanging off the side of Mount Rushmore, Phineas gripped his safety line in one hand and his pickax in the other. He gazed up at the towering stretch of granite. "Now, where should we start?"

Ferb swung from his own safety line, jack-hammer in hand. But before he could answer, a familiar voice called to them from below.

"Hi, Phineas!" their friend Isabella shouted. Phineas squinted. She was so far below them, she looked like an Isabella-shaped bug. "Whatcha doin'?"

"It's a surprise!" Phineas shouted back.

"Can I help?" Isabella was always helpful when it came to Phineas and Ferb's plans. And she always

29

seemed to turn up at just the right moment. Her Fireside Girl friends could be helpful, too.

Phineas thought for a second. "We could use a lookout," he yelled, already turning his back to her. He had a masterpiece to finish.

"You got it!" Isabella raced toward the tallest tree she could find. She scrambled up the trunk, pulling herself onto a high, sturdy branch. Her legs firmly planted on the bark, she pulled out her walkie-talkie and called her troop of Fireside Girls.

Isabella was always prepared. For anything. Because when you were friends with Phineas, *anything* tended to happen a lot.

Chapter 5

Miles and miles beneath Isabella and her Fireside Girls, Perry the Platypus's digging machine tunneled toward the center of the earth. Dr. Doofenshmirtz's huge Drill-a-nator may have been fast, but Agent P was faster. As soon as he'd been left alone, Perry had gotten back into his drill and had taken off in hot pursuit of the evil scientist. Soon the platypus had closed the distance between them, and before

Dr. D even knew he was being followed, Perry had drilled right through the roof of the Drill-a-nator. Catching the mad inventor by  surprise, Agent P scrambled out of his own drill and lunged toward Dr. Doofenshmirtz.

Perry knocked the fiendish scientist to the floor and seized control of the steering wheel. He was just in time—the Drill-a-Nator was drilling straight toward a bottomless pit of lava!

HULL OVERHEATING, the computer warned, as they drew closer and closer to the lava. HULL OVERHEATING.

"The molten lava at the earth's core completely slipped my mind," Dr. Doofenshmirtz admitted in a panicky voice.

Perry wasn't surprised. He yanked the

steering wheel hard to the left, sending them back toward the surface.

"Oh, no!" Dr. Doofenshmirtz cried. He was huddling in a corner, wishing he had never built this stupid machine in the first place. "The lava is following us!"

Perry swung around to peer through the back window. A river of fire was chasing them through the tunnel. Soon they would be incinerated!

Perry thought fast. He set his own digging machine on autopilot and released it into the tunnel. The machine dug a tunnel that

branched off from the
main tunnel and carved a
new path for the lava—a
path *away* from the Drill-a-
nator.

Dr. Doofenshmirtz cheered Perry on. The
two mortal enemies were on the same side.
"The lava is being diverted," he reported with
relief. "You did it, Perry the Platypus. You
saved us!"

But just as Agent P was about to relax,
he saw a terrifying sight. The other digging
machine had tunneled around in a circle—it
was about to intercept the Drill-a-nator's tunnel. And that meant . . .

"I hate to be a stickler," Dr. Doofenshmirtz
shrieked, "but the lava is
coming again!"

As the mad scientist
trembled uselessly in the
corner, Perry pushed the

Drill-a-nator faster and faster. The machine began to shake and quake as it moved mounds of earth out of its way. Perry began to fear it would fall to pieces before they could reach the surface. If that happened, they would be instantly crushed by tons of rock and dirt.

Unless the flood of burning lava got them first.

Chapter 6

Back on the earth's surface, Candace had no idea her brother's pet platypus was in such danger. Although if she had known, she probably wouldn't have had time to care. She had problems of her own—and one problem in particular. Her brother.

Linda was back in the gift shop, and she wasn't going anywhere. Candace had tried whining and wheedling, sulking and begging.

She'd tried everything—but none of it convinced her mother to leave.

The gangly boy behind the cash register watched suspiciously as Linda examined a thick, wooden walking stick.

"Uh, ma'am," the boy said nervously, his voice cracking, "if ya handle the big stick, ya gotta buy it."

Candace tugged at her mother, forcing her to drop the stick. "Mom! You gotta see what Phineas and Ferb are doing!" she urged her, more desperate than ever.

Linda heaved a sigh. Looking at souvenirs wasn't nearly as much fun with Candace constantly babbling about Phineas and Ferb. So she shrugged and

agreed to leave the gift shop—temporarily, at least.

Phineas and Ferb were racing the clock. They just *had* to finish before Candace saw what they were up to. Which meant they had no time for the meddling park ranger who spotted them hanging from the monument.

"Uh, excuse me," he shouted through his megaphone, gaping up at the two boys dangling from George Washington's forehead. "Aren't you boys a little young to be restoring a national monument?"

Phineas switched off his jackhammer and Ferb held a megaphone to his mouth. "Yes. Yes, we are."

The park ranger shrugged, then grinned. "Well, it's good to see young people taking an interest in our national heritage," he said cheerfully. He hopped in his jeep and drove away—and the brothers got back to work.

But all too soon, their time ran out. "She's coming!" Isabella shouted from her lookout post.

The boys were so close to finishing their secret project—but not close enough. Dangling from ropes hundreds of feet above the ground, they hammered and  drilled and carved and sanded as fast as they could.

"She's getting closer!" Isabella warned them.

"We're running a little behind schedule!" Phineas shouted back. "Let's go to Plan B!"

Isabella hoisted her walkie-talkie. "Plan B, girls!" she alerted her Fireside troop.

The girls sprang into action. They pulled a thick rope and dragged a giant piece of canvas into place, blocking the view of the monument from the observation deck. Now anyone standing on the deck wouldn't see the mountain. They would just see what the girls had painted on the giant canvas: an exact replica of Mount Rushmore.

Isabella crossed her fingers. Now there was nothing left to do but wait, watch, and hope it would work.

"You are gonna be *shocked* by what I'm about to show you, Mom," Candace said as she towed her mother up the long, steep staircase leading to the observation deck.

But when they got to the top, Phineas and Ferb were safely hidden behind the Mount Rushmore tarp. It was almost as good as real life. Almost.

"Hmm," Linda said, taking her first look at the monument. (Or, at least, what she *thought* was the monument.) "I guess some things look better in photos."

Candace stared at the mountain in confusion. Where were Phineas and Ferb? How had they managed to escape *again*?

Linda's cell phone rang. Candace could hear her stepdad's voice blaring through the tiny speaker.

"Hi, honey," he said. "I found an absolutely brilliant parking space!"

Candace smirked. She knew what that meant. "Absolutely brilliant" was dad-code for "a million miles away from the entrance."

"Great!" Linda said. She wasn't quite as good at deciphering dad-code. "I'll meet you  at the gift shop, dear! I still have to buy that big stick."

Candace groaned. Back to the gift shop, *again*? Candace was about to take off after her—when a bird flew straight into the giant piece of canvas!

The canvas Mount Rushmore toppled over, revealing the real mountain.

"Huh?" Candace muttered, confused. The right half of the mountain was draped in a massive sheet. Two small figures dangled on either side of it. Candace squinted. Was that . . . ? It was! Candace clenched her fists. Now she had proof that Phineas and Ferb were up on the mountain—and her mom was nowhere in sight.

"Now!" Phineas shouted. His voice echoed across the ragged peaks.

Phineas and Ferb swung down on their ropes, whipping the sheet off the mountain.

Candace gasped. Next to the familiar four presidents, there was now a fifth face. A twisted, deformed, disgusting face. It looked kind of like Candace—if she had morphed into a monstrous freak.

Ferb glanced up at the face and realized the grand masterpiece required one little finishing touch. He heaved his pickax and smashed it into a rock at the base of the mountain. A giant crack appeared in the rock face, and spread upward to the very top of the monument. With a thunderous blast, the twisted face shuddered and burst. Rock fragments spattered the ground. Gradually, the dust cleared, revealing a new face in the granite.

It was Candace's face, pretty and perfect and towering thousands of feet above the ground.

Candace had never seen anything like it.

"Why, it's—it's *beautiful*." Tears of joy trickled down her cheeks as she stared up at herself, immortalized in stone. She whirled around, racing down the stairs and calling frantically for her mother. This was the most amazing thing ever. Her mother had to see it right away. "Mom, I've got to show you something right now!" she shouted. "Come on, follow me!"

"Candace, are you still trying to get the boys in trouble?" Linda asked wearily, staring at the hundreds of steps.

"No, no, no!" Candace cried. "This is a great thing!" She still couldn't believe what her brothers had done for her. Especially after all the times she'd tried to get them in trouble. "It's the nicest thing anyone has ever done for me!"

Her mom trudged back up to the observation deck, moaning with every step. It was taking *forever*. "You know, Candace, this is the *third* time I've climbed up here," she complained. "I'm already down half a dress size!"

"Come on!" Candace called from the top of the steps. She could hardly wait for her mother to join her. "Hurry!"

Chapter 7

Candace had her back to the monument, so she didn't see the Drill-a-nator explode out of the mountain and into the air. Perry and Dr. Doofenshmirtz had made it back to the surface, and not a moment too soon. Perry fiddled with the controls, setting a course for Old Reliable geyser.

They plunged toward the earth at almost a hundred miles per hour. Dr. Doofenshmirtz

screamed in terror—then in rage, as Agent P released a parachute and floated to safety.

The parachute-less Dr. Doofenshmirtz rocketed toward the geyser and crashed into the water. For a moment, all was silent and still. He poked his head above the surface. "I'm okay," he said, surprised to discover he was still alive. "I—"

The geyser erupted.

"Fie upon you, Perry the Platypus!" But his screams were drowned out by the thunder of the water, as it burst out of the ground and swept him away.

* * *

Candace didn't notice any of it. She was still glaring down at her slow-moving mother. "Hurry, Mom! You won't believe it."

Finally, Candace got tired of waiting. She ran across the observation deck to catch another glimpse of her mountain-sized birthday surprise.

She got a surprise all right—just not the one she'd been expecting.

Before her eyes, a gush of molten lava shot out of Candace's stone nose. The river of lava was rising through the Drill-a-nator tunnel— and nothing could stop it now!

"Ew!" Candace squealed in disgust as a red

rivulet burst out of the statue's forehead. Two streams gushed out of the stone chin, and a third dribbled down the monument's cheek. It looked like the mountainous face was covered in a rash of exploding pimples.

The perfectly sculpted face began to crumble into molten debris just as Old Reliable geyser spit up a towering flume of water. Shooting higher than ever before, the water doused the lava and the mountain disappeared behind a gigantic cloud of steam.

As the steam faded away, Candace's mouth dropped open in horror.

"Whew, finally made it, honey," her mom said cheerfully, joining her at the railing. "Now, what is it you wanted me to see?"

"B-b-b-but . . ." Candace couldn't believe it. The face—*her* face—was completely gone. There was nothing left of her birthday surprise but a bare sheet of granite.

"You're right, it's beautiful!" Linda cried, as she got her first look at the *real* Mount Rushmore. "Happy birthday, honey." She threw her arms around Candace and gave her a kiss on the forehead.

Candace just stood there, limp in her arms. She was too shocked to speak.

"Now, let's go find your father." Linda hurried off, but Candace didn't move. Not even when Phineas and Ferb showed up.

"Did ya like your birthday present?" Phineas asked.

Candace just whimpered. It was the best she could do.

 51

Ferb shrugged. "Well, it was definitely better than the gorilla in the cake."

Exhausted, Candace wandered away from her brothers. Some birthday.

She stumbled down the stairs, her eyes fixed on the ground. She didn't see Jeremy coming toward her, looking cuter than ever. "Hey, Candace!" he called out, catching sight of her.

At the sound of his voice, Candace looked up.

Looking a little nervous, Jeremy handed her a box wrapped in a purple ribbon. "I had a break and I, uh, I thought I'd give this to you for your birthday."

Jeremy gave me a present! she thought, and suddenly she wasn't tired anymore. She felt like jumping up and down, screaming and shouting and dancing. But instead she just said, "Thank you" and unwrapped the box.

"I saw you looking at it in the gift shop," Jeremy explained as Candace pulled out her present.

"A Mount Rushmore bobble head." Candace stared down at the wobbling presidents.

"Y-y-you like it?" Jeremy asked. Now *he* was blushing.

Like it?

On the one hand, it was the lamest souvenir on earth. It looked even lamer up close.

On the other hand, she thought, Jeremy gave me a present!

"I absolutely love it!" she exclaimed, hugging it to her chest.

"Great!" Jeremy's face lit up with a smile. Candace felt like she was glowing. "I gotta get back," he said. "Happy birthday!"

This was the happiest birthday ever, Candace thought, squeezing her beloved bobble heads.

Part Two

Chapter 1

Phineas and Ferb were having a pretty ordinary summer so far. They'd built a rocket. Tracked down Frankenstein's brain. And then there was the afternoon they climbed the Eiffel Tower.

You know: same old, same old.

But then came a day guaranteed to be different. Phineas knew it as soon as he woke up. There was something *special* about this day. Something exciting . . . but what?

"Mi, mi, mi, mi." Candace's voice floated into the room from down the hall. She was singing in her bedroom. "La, la, la, la."

Phineas sat up in bed. This was seriously *weird*. "Ferb, are you hearing what I'm hearing? Candace singing early in the morning."

Ferb just looked confused. Obviously he didn't get it either. Or maybe he wasn't quite awake yet.

Phineas jumped out of bed. He and his brother crept down the hall to Candace's room. Candace was playing her guitar and scribbling lyrics on a sheet of music.

"Mom, it's your birthday," Candace sang. "Thanks for all the care and love you give." She scribbled down the words. "Eh, yeah. Yeah, that's all right," she muttered to herself. "I like that. *Mom, it's your birthday.*"

Phineas gaped at his brother, horrified. "It's Mom's birthday! How could we forget Mom's birthday? Where have all the days gone?"

Ferb didn't answer. But if he *had*, he might have reminded Phineas exactly where all the days had gone.

There was the day they built a roller coaster. ("We can't forget Mom's birthday!" Phineas had shouted as they zoomed down the track.)

There was the day they'd rustled a herd of cattle. ("We can't forget Mom's birthday!" Phineas had cried, keeping a tight grip on his cowboy hat so the wind wouldn't blow it away.)

There was the day they'd surfed a tidal wave. ("We can't forget Mom's birthday!" Phineas exclaimed, hanging ten.) There was the day they'd turned into rock stars, the day they'd found some dinosaurs, the day they'd—well, you get the idea.

Now Mom's birthday was finally here.

And they had both forgotten.

"We should do something nice for Mom," Phineas said, "what with Dad being out of town on business and all."

Ferb nodded. Then he waited. He knew his brother would come up with an idea.

Suddenly, Phineas snapped his fingers. "I got an idea!"

And it was brilliant.

Candace carried a breakfast tray into her mother's room. She was determined to give her mom the greatest birthday ever. "Eggs and bacon, oh, yeah," she sang quietly to herself.

Linda was still sleeping. A framed picture of her husband lay on the pillow beside her. Candace took a deep breath, ready to wake her up with an awesome birthday surprise. "Mom, let me be the first to say—"

"Happy birthday, Mom!" Phineas shouted, barreling into the room. He flung the door open wide—so wide that it smashed Candace and her breakfast surprise right into the wall.

SPLAT!

Phineas hurried to his mom's bedside. Ferb followed, wheeling a tray covered with a white tablecloth. A pot of coffee sat on top.

"We brought you some periodicals to read," Phineas said eagerly, handing Linda a stack of magazines. "Like *Mom Daily, Mom Weekly, Mom Bi-Weekly.* And"—Phineas gave Ferb a silent signal, and Ferb poured a mug of freshly ground coffee—"just the way you like it, a half-cap, double frappé, mocha-choca-latte, mezzo espresso," Phineas said proudly.

Linda glowed. "Oh, wow! You boys really outdid yourselves."

"*Au contraire, ma mère,*" Phineas said in a fake French accent. "I declare it is our mission to give you the best birthday ever!" He pushed her sleep mask back down over her eyes. "So relax, and no peeking till we come get you."

Phineas and Ferb bustled out of the room. Their mom settled back into bed, smiling. "Oh, those boys are too much," she murmured. Then she sniffed the air. "Mmmm! Oh, I smell bacon and eggs."

What she smelled was Candace, who was covered in food.

Candace peeled herself off the wall and slunk out of the room. She promised herself she would find another way to celebrate her mom's birthday.

Somehow.

Chapter 2

Down in the kitchen, Phineas and Ferb were preparing a birthday breakfast extravaganza.

"Thank you, Mrs. Garcia-Shapiro," Phineas said into the tiny phone hooked on his ear. "We appreciate you helping us out. Oop, another call." As he switched over to the other line, Phineas began dumping coins out of his piggy bank. He was an expert at multitasking. "Talk to me, Buford, my man."

While Phineas listened to Buford, Ferb was

tidying up an omelet station. He wore an apron, a chef's hat, and a fake mustache—the perfect uniform for a birthday omelet chef.

"Thanks, Buford," Phineas said into the phone. "Glad we can count on you."

Everything was falling into place.

"Ahem!" Candace appeared in the doorway, clearing her throat loudly.

"Hey, Candace!" Phineas was glad to see his big sister. After all, planning a big birthday breakfast was a *big* job. He and Ferb could use her help. "Wanna man the omelet station for Mom's birthday?"

Candace scowled. "I'm doing my own thing."

She waited for her brothers to react.

"Well, aren't you going ask me what it is?" she asked finally.

Phineas shrugged. "Sure. Uh, what are you doing?"

"It's a *secret!*" Candace said smugly. She stormed off, hoping they wouldn't figure out the catch with her secret plan: she still didn't have one.

She shouldn't have worried. Phineas didn't wonder why his sister was acting weird.

Besides, he had a birthday breakfast surprise to plan. He and Ferb and Perry the Platypus had plenty of stuff to do. Speaking of their pet—

Phineas looked around the kitchen. He and Ferb were alone.

"Hey, where's Perry?" Phineas asked.

Little did he know that Perry had a secret of his own. . . .

While Phineas and Ferb were busy in the kitchen, Perry had slipped into the hallway to stand in front of a photo of himself. He wasn't admiring how handsome he looked—which was very—he was on a mission.

He spun the photo upside down, and a secret passageway opened in the wall. Perry ducked inside and whooshed through a tube that led straight to his secret underground lair. Down there, he could ditch the dumb-platypus act. Phineas and Ferb would never know that their pet was really the smartest, slyest platypus on earth: Agent P.

Agent P dropped into his command-center chair, just in time to receive an urgent message from his boss, Major Monogram.

"Morning, Agent P," the major said brusquely. "Seventeen minutes ago, our spy satellites located Doofenshmirtz. He's hiding out in his mountaintop-castle laboratory." An image of Doofenshmirtz's castle popped up on the screen. It was an isolated fortress, just right for an evil madman.

The major continued, "He's purchased some suspicious items over the Internet, including a giant metal sphere and two animatronic wax robots."

"Gosh, those things give me the creeps," the major complained. "The way they're all robotic and waxy. Ugh! They—"

Agent P knew what he had to do and there

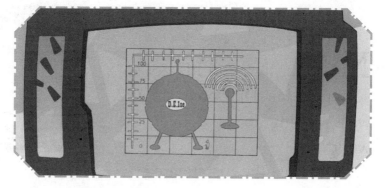

wasn't time to listen to the major describe his fear of wax-covered robots. He pressed a button on his chair and it transformed into a jet pack, blasting him out of the room. The major kept babbling, but Perry was already gone, hot on the trail of the evil Dr. Doofenshmirtz.

When it came to saving the world, there wasn't a second to waste.

69

* * *

Not so far away, in his not-so-secret evil lair, Dr. Doofenshmirtz was plotting to take over the world.

Or at least the tristate area.

"Ah, *The Unicorn Whisperer*, the feel-good movie of the year," he murmured, dusting off a copy of the gruesomely pink DVD before putting it back on its display table. "And soon it will be gone!" He belted out an evil laugh—then choked, as Agent P leaped through the window.

Dr. Doofenshmirtz widened his eyes in exaggerated surprise. "Oh, no! It's Perry the Platypus!" Then the evil scientist burst into laughter. "Ha! I fooled you, Perry the Platypus!" he cried. "I'm not really scared. I'm not scared because I have a new security system. Voilà!" Dr. Doofenshmirtz chuckled as he pressed a button on a tiny remote control.

A giant door in the wall opened and two animatronic wax robots lurched into the room. One was dressed like Abraham Lincoln, the other like George Washington—and *both* were heading straight for Perry.

"Do you like them, Perry the Platypus?" Dr. Doofenshmirtz asked, obviously delighted by his new toys.

"Get him," said the George Washington robot in a mechanical monotone.

"I got them very cheap from a wax museum that went bankrupt." Dr. Doofenshmirtz giggled. "I love it when dreams fail."

Before Perry could react, Lincoln grabbed the platypus's right hand and his right foot. Washington grabbed his left hand and his left foot. Then the robotic presidents stretched out Agent P flat as a platypus pancake, and they lifted him several feet off the floor. Perry squirmed and struggled, but it was no use. He was trapped!

Dr. Doofenshmirtz paced back and forth in front of the captive agent. "As you know, I've been trying to take over the tristate area for quite some time now, and I realized this tri-state area is filled with things I detest."

"So many things," Dr. Doofenshmirtz fumed, pausing in front of a red, blinking arrow. "Like blinking traffic arrows. Stop blinking at me, telling me where to go!" he shout-ed. "Point. Point. Point. Oooh, I hate you!"

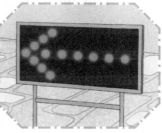

Before he could get too distracted by its detestableness, he moved on. "Let's see. What else? Ear hair." He pointed at a giant clump of ear hair trapped under a glass dome. "Oh, yes, I've always hated you."

Next up was a large white

bird, chained to a table. "Pelicans, terrible creatures," Dr. Doofenshmirtz complained, keeping a safe distance from the beast. "What are you, a bird or a garbage disposal?"

The final display table held a set of bagpipes, a banjo, and some bongos. "Ugh, musical instruments that start with the letter *b*." Dr. Doofenshmirtz shivered in horror. "You get the idea. It's a long list. I've been working on it a while." He rubbed his hands together in evil anticipation. "Anyway, I realized I should build something that would make all those awful things disappear. Behold, Perry the Platypus. . . . Shrink Spheria!"

Looking outside, Perry could see a giant metal sphere that stood almost thirty feet high. A long antenna jutted out the top. The doctor glanced quickly at Perry to see his reaction. But the platypus's face was blank.

"You like it?" Dr. Doofenshmirtz asked hopefully. "I was going to call it a Shrinkinator, but I've done that whole 'inator' thing before. It's just been done to death."

Perry just stared at him.

Disgusted, Dr. Doofenshmirtz decided to show Agent P a simulation of how his invention worked. "Bring him over here," he commanded his robots.

The presidents carried Perry over to a large computer suspended from the ceiling. Dr. Doofenshmirtz carefully typed out a word on the giant keyboard: P-E-L-I-C-A-N

"Pelican," he said, as a picture of a pelican popped up on the screen. "Shrink Spheria homes in on its molecular structure, and then turns all the particles into *sparticles*, thereby shrinking it into a teeny, tiny speck, so small I never have to see it again!"

On the screen, a mini Shrink Spheria shot out glowing, green shrink rays at the picture of the pelican. The bird turned green—then shrank and shrank. And shrank—until it disappeared.

"So, good-bye to you, Perry the Platypus," Dr. Doofenshmirtz said, cackling. Then he turned his back on the spy and his waxy captors. "Enjoy your *presidential* suite." He hurried out of the room, eager to rid the world of detestable detour signs and irritating musical instruments beginning with *b*. By the time he was finished, he planned to shrink down anything and everything the tristate area cherished.

And Agent P could do nothing but watch.

Chapter 3

Candace's desk was a mess.

Okay, that wasn't particularly unusual.

But what *was* unusual was that the mess was made up of art supplies. In the center of it all sat Candace, who was putting the finishing touches on a new birthday surprise.

"The boys may have won breakfast," she said to the empty room, "but wait'll Mom sees this homemade birthday card."

She took one last look at her masterpiece,

then signed it with a flourish:

Love, the child who loves you most,
Candace

Candace proudly carried her card down-stairs. She almost ran into Phineas and Ferb, who were leading their blindfolded mother down the hall. Quietly, Candace followed them.

"All right, Mom, almost there," Phineas said, guiding Linda toward the kitchen.

"Oh, this is so exciting!" she cried.

"Okay, you can look!"

Linda pulled off her blindfold and gasped in delight. Her friends and all the neighborhood kids crowded around a table piled high with her favorite foods. Banners and streamers dangled from the ceiling, and balloons bobbed over their heads.

"Happy birthday!" everyone shouted.

Everyone but Candace. She stood silently behind her mother, waiting to be noticed.

"What a beautiful breakfast!" her mother exclaimed.

"Mom?" Candace said quietly. But no one heard her.

She gripped her homemade card tighter. "Mom, this may not be a fantastic breakfast, but—"

"Ladies and gentlemen," Phineas announced loudly. "Mom's birthday card!"

The crowd *oohed* and *aahed* as Buford toted out a giant birthday card and placed it under a spotlight. Phineas and Ferb joined him in front of the card. It was twice as tall as they were.

"It may be big," Candace reassured herself, "but it's *bo*-ring!"

After all, the front of the card was totally empty except for the words *To Mom*, drawn in wobbly handwriting. What kind of card was that?

Then Phineas opened it.

A whole world of 3-D birthday excitement popped out. There was a giant cake that looked ready to eat. Streamers shot into the air, candles twinkled, and sparklers sparkled.

"Oh, boys, I can't believe you two made it yourselves!" their mom gushed.

Candace couldn't believe it either. The card was amazing. Compared to that, her little card was . . .

Bo-ring.

Candace's eye started to twitch. It tended to do that when Phineas got the best of her. (It twitched a *lot*.) Her card was just embarrassing. Quick, before her mom could see it, Candace tore the card into tiny pieces.

And then, just to be safe, she ate it.

"Glad you liked the card, Mom," Phineas said. Behind him, Candace fumed.

Ferb gave his mother a modest smile. "It's a

simple, postmodern fusion of origami and pop-up."

"Yeah! And just wait till you see your present!" Phineas grabbed Ferb, and they dashed out of the room to prepare yet another birthday treat.

Candace sighed miserably.

"Oh, I hope the boys don't go overboard with my present." Linda sounded worried. "All I'd really like is that dress from the cute little sundress shop."

Candace felt like a lightbulb had just popped over her head. No, not a lightbulb—a

giant, blazing sun. "You mean that really cute one with the polka dots?" she asked eagerly.

Before her mother had finished nodding, Candace was out the door. She hopped on her bike, slapped on her shiny purple helmet, and took off down the street.

"I know what she wants!" she cried, pedaling as fast as she could. Candace leaned over the handlebars and tore through the neighborhood, heading for the center of town. "Cute little sundress!" she shouted, panting as she pedaled faster and faster. "Cute little sundress! Cute little sundress!"

Chapter 4

Candace was almost as excited about her secret plan as Dr. Doofenshmirtz was about his. He gazed at his Shrink Spheria with awe. This time, his plan was going to work. He was sure of it.

"Hey, Perry the Platypus!" he shouted. "Say good-bye to blinking detour signs, forever!" Shaking with evil laughter, he pressed a button on his control panel. The antenna on the giant sphere began to glow. Orange waves of light rippled out of the antenna, spreading through the castle.

Agent P's eyes widened as the orange waves hit the blinking detour sign. It shrank down to a speck . . . then disappeared!

"Yes, I'm an evil genius!" Dr. Doofenshmirtz shouted. "Now I have to wait four minutes for it to recharge, which isn't so bad. I think I'll go with pelicans next. What do you think, Perry the Platypus? Pelicans next?"

Perry ignored Dr. Doofenshmirtz's evil taunting. He had a plan of his own. But first, he had to escape from the wax presidents.

A circular wooden candelabra hung above Perry's head. While Dr. Doofenshmirtz ranted outside, Perry twisted around and used his mouth to retrieve the blow dart he'd hidden away in his fur for emergencies.

He knew he had only one shot.

Holding the blow dart in his bill, he took aim at the frayed rope that held the candelabra—and blew.

The dart sliced through the rope, and the candelabra crashed to the floor, surrounding Perry and the wax presidents in a ring of fire. The effect of the heat from the candles on the wax robots was evident immediately.

"I cannot tell a lie," the Washington robot moaned, shrinking from the flames as the wax dripped off his face, "I'm melting!"

In moments, the robots' faces and bodies had melted into a mess on the floor. They collapsed into a jumbled heap of sticky machine parts. Wax Lincoln's head toppled off and rolled into the wall, his stovepipe hat still firmly in place.

Perry raced out the door, determined to stop Dr. Doofenshmirtz before he could do any more harm.

But Dr. Doofenshmirtz had already done enough.

The Shrink Spheria ray was more powerful

than even he knew. The shrinking waves had penetrated the castle—then kept going, rippling across town and shrinking every blinking detour sign they passed. Including one sign that sat in front of a gaping pothole in Argyle Street, preventing local traffic from driving into it.

When the sign disappeared, cars and trucks had no way of knowing they should take a detour. Among the many vehicles affected by this was a truck from the Live Moth Circus. (You may not be familiar with the Live Moth Circus, but the name pretty much says it all.) It drove right down Argyle Street—and right into the hole.

As it crashed into the hole, the doors of the circus truck flew open and the Live Moth Circus fluttered into the air, free at last.

Free moths are hungry moths, and eating is what moths do best. The circus moths flew about searching for fabric to munch.

Candace had just left the Cute L'il Sundress

Shoppe, the purple polka-dotted sundress her mother wanted in hand. Hunched over her handlebars, eyes narrowed, Candace pedaled faster than she had ever pedaled before. "Cute little sundress," she muttered through gritted teeth. "Cute little sundress. Cute little sundress."

This *had* to work.

Candace was totally focused on the road ahead of her and completely unaware of the swarm of moths devouring the dress behind her.

She burst into the backyard, the sundress hanger hidden behind her back. She wanted the gift to be a surprise. "Hey, everybody!

Look what . . ." Her voice trailed off. Phineas and Ferb were putting on a fashion show. The whole neighborhood was in the audience—including her mom. Linda sat in a homemade throne, wearing a birthday crown.

"You gotta be kidding me," Candace muttered. No one noticed her. As usual.

"Our first supermodel sports a chic, stylin', not-couture sundress," Phineas announced as a long-legged model strutted down the stage. "Perfect for our birthday queen to sip iced lattes while enjoying a fabu day in the sun."

"Huh." Candace felt a little better when she saw the model was wearing a yellow dress. "Well, they have the wrong sundress. It's okay,

but it is not as great as *this*!"

She whipped out the sundress—at least, she tried to. But the dress was long gone. She was holding nothing but a hanger, surrounded by a dress-shaped swarm of fluttering moths!

Chapter 5

Now that the blinking detour signs had been vanquished (along with Candace's birthday present), Dr. Doofenshmirtz was ready to move on to his next target.

"Yoo-hoo, Mr. Pelican!" he shouted gleefully. "I'm going to shrink you now!" Giggling, he pressed the PELICAN button on his control panel.

Nothing happened.

He pressed it again, then again, jabbing

it harder each time.

Still nothing.

"Why is it not working?" he wondered aloud. "Something's blocking the—" His jaw dropped as he realized the truth. It wasn't *something*. It was *someone*.

Someone named Agent P.

After dealing with the wax presidents, Perry had climbed to the top of the Shrink Spheria. He was tugging at the tall antenna, trying to snap it off.

"Hey!" Enraged, Dr. Doofenshmirtz swung the arm of the cherry picker toward the platypus. Holding tight, Perry swung himself around the antenna once, twice, three times, then let go at exactly the right moment. Momentum carried him through the air and he slammed right into Dr. Doofenshmirtz.

The evil madman stumbled into his control panel, accidentally activating the Shrink

Spheria's shrinking ray. "Oh, well," Dr. Doofenshmirtz said, shrugging. So things weren't shrinking in the order he'd planned. Worse things had happened. "Good-bye to musical instruments that start with *b*."

At that exact moment, Candace was running away from the swarm of moths. She ducked into her bedroom and slammed the door shut behind her, finally safe.

Safe, but still no closer to giving her mother the perfect birthday surprise.

"Wait a minute!" she exclaimed as an idea popped into her head. Why hadn't she thought of this before? "I can still give Mom the one thing that the boys can't. The gift of music. Played on my friend, the bass."

She grabbed her trusty bass guitar and began playing the song she'd written for her mother. But before she got out the second note, Dr. D's shrinking ray penetrated her house and hit her bass guitar.

That's *bass*. An instrument that starts with *b*.

It shrank down to a speck and disappeared.

Candace looked down at her empty hands in confusion. "Oh, well." She shrugged and grabbed another instrument from her collection. "It's a good thing I play the banjo!"

As she touched it, so did the shrinking ray—it disappeared.

Candace grabbed for another instrument. "It's a good thing I play the bassoon."

That disappeared, too.

"It's a good thing I play the bugle!"

It vanished into thin air.

"It's a good thing I play the bongos!"

Gone.

"It's a good thing I play the balalaika!" Candace was getting desperate. She held tight . . . but not tight enough.

"It's a good thing I play the bagpipes—"

They were gone before she even got the words out. And that was her very last instrument. Candace felt like a popped balloon: totally deflated. She sighed. "I should've manned the omelet station."

* * *

D r. Doofenshmirtz leaped onto the top of the sphere, but Perry was hot on his tail. They chased each other around and around, but it was no use. They were too evenly matched.

Suddenly, they heard a familiar robotic voice. "A house divided cannot stand." It was the robot Abraham Lincoln. He was back—and he wasn't alone!

"Yeah, what he said," robot George Washington agreed.

The heat had melted the wax, but when it cooled the two robots had fused into one. Now there was one angry robot with two very angry heads.

The two-headed robot climbed into the cherry-picker bucket and raised itself level with Dr. Doofenshmirtz and Perry.

Dr. Doofenshmirtz cackled with glee. "Oh, Perry the Platypus, you melted their wax, but you can never melt what's inside: *pure evil.*"

The robot jumped onto the sphere—and crashed through the thin metal surface. It plummeted down, smashing the power source at the heart of the device.

KABOOOOOOM!

The Shrink Spheria exploded!

Perry and Dr. Doofenshmirtz shot straight up into the air, blown sky-high by the force of the explosion. "I should've seen that coming," Dr. Doofenshmirtz groaned.

Perry, Dr. Doofenshmirtz, and the two-headed robot rocketed up and up and up. But what goes up must come down—and they were all going to come down *hard*.

All of them, that is, except for Perry. He tugged a cord and released his hidden parachute, waving good-bye as he gently floated away from Dr. Doofenshmirtz and his evil robot.

"Curse you, Perry the Platypus!" the madman shouted as he plummeted toward the earth.

Perry smirked. Mission accomplished.

Chapter 6

The birthday breakfast had gone *splat*.

The card had been torn into a million pieces.

The cute little sundress was moth food.

And the birthday song was a total bust.

Candace realized it was over. She was out of ideas and out of options. There was nothing left to do but give up.

She forced herself to go back outside. The fashion show was over. But there was still a crowd of people sitting in the grass, staring up at the huge, blank screen that hung over the empty stage.

"Candace, honey, come join us," Linda urged. She was kneeling on a picnic blanket with Phineas and Ferb. "The boys have put together a little video."

Candace trudged over to join her brothers. She had to admit it: Phineas and Ferb had given their mom the greatest birthday ever.

"Here, you can do the honors." Phineas handed her a remote control.

"Fine. Whatever." Candace hit PLAY.

The giant screen flickered to life. "Happy birthday, Mom," Phineas's voice-over said. "From birth to young adult to mid-sized adult, from the '80s to the '90s, Mom enchants everyone she meets." Even Candace couldn't help smiling at the photos—there was Mom as a baby, Mom in '80s workout gear, Mom in '90s grunge. It was so weird to see Mom as anything but . . . well, Mom.

"But who is this person we call Mom?" the voice-over asked. "A true testament to what a great mom you are is that your daughter would take the time to write . . . this song."

What? Candace's eyes widened. That was *her* up on the screen, singing the song she'd written. Phineas and Ferb must have filmed her that morning while she was rehearsing.

103

"Mom, it's your birthday," the on-screen Candace sang.

"Nice song, Sis," Phineas murmured.

Candace blushed. But she had to admit she sounded pretty good.

"Thanks for all the care and love you give.

Not to mention the meals.

Sometimes I get kinda nervous,

And forget to tell you how I feel."

"Come on," Phineas said, tugging his sister toward the stage.

Candace felt a little weird singing in front of all those people—but after all, this was *her* song. *Her* birthday surprise. She grabbed a microphone and started singing along with herself.

And it felt great.

" 'I'm a little high-strung,' " she sang.

" 'It's just because I'm young.

" 'Mom, I adore ya,

" 'And I'll do anything for ya.' "

Phineas had set up his DJ equipment at the edge of the stage. He sat down at his console and began scratching some records along with the music, while Ferb took over on drums. Even Isabella's Fireside Girls left the audience to climb onstage and get in the act as backup singers.

"'Although my brothers make me frantic,'" Candace sang, throwing everything she had into the music.

"'With every single crazy antic
And when I'm bouncing off the walls,
You're the one who stays calm.'"

"'You're the one who stays calm,'" Phineas and Ferb chimed in.

"'Because you love me for who I am,'" Candace finished, "'I'll always love you, Mom.'"

They got a standing ovation. And, for once, Candace didn't mind sharing the spotlight. She finally understood that it didn't matter whose present was the best, as long as their mom was happy.

And Linda had never looked happier.

"What a beautiful song, honey," Linda said, wiping away a tear.

Candace beamed. "Well, I really wanted you to have a happy birth—"

"Oh! I almost forgot!" Phineas cut in. He grabbed his mom and tugged her toward a big-screen TV sitting at the other end of the yard. "We set up a satellite uplink with Dad."

"Ooh, a satellite uplink!" she squealed.

Candace was forgotten all over again. But this time, she didn't mind. Because Candace just wanted her mom to have the best birthday ever, and that meant getting to spend time with the whole family. She just wished that *she* had thought of the satellite hookup.

But since she hadn't, she was glad that Phineas and Ferb had. Candace hated to admit it, but sometimes her brothers were actually kind of useful to have around.

Candace's stepdad appeared on the screen. "Hello, love," he said, waving at his wife. "Happy birthday."

"Hi, honey," she said eagerly. "I miss you. And you're missing the festivities. The boys threw me the greatest party, and Candace wrote me this really amazing song. Can you hear me?"

As Candace watched her mother chatter away about all the birthday excitement, Perry the Platypus came up to join her.

"Oh, hey, Perry. Where've you been?" She was in such a good mood that she was almost glad to see him. "You missed all the fun."

Of course, Perry didn't say anything. Agent P was back in disguise as a dumb pet platypus. And he would stay that way . . . until the next time he was needed to save the world.

Or at least the tristate area.

Don't miss the fun in the next
Phineas & Ferb book...

Thrill-o-rama!

Adapted by Kitty Richards
Based on the series created by Dan Povenmire & Jeff "Swampy" Marsh

Candace sat in her pink bedroom, a banana to her ear, as she pretended to call her not-so-secret crush, Jeremy Johnson. "Hello," she began, "is this the Johnson residence? I'd like to speak to Jeremy Johnson." She smiled. "This is Candace Flynn. Why am I calling, you ask?" She referred to her open notebook, which listed several reasons for calling. She chose one. "Because I have a question about our algebra assignment. Thank you, I'll hold." She frantically flipped through her notebook.

Okay, okay. Let's see . . . opening jokes, opening jokes . . . "Hey-ah, Jeremy. This is Candace Flynn. So, what do you get when you cross a yak and a Martian?"

Just then, her bedroom door opened with a squeak. "Honey," said a voice, "could I interrupt for just a sec?"

"Why, Jeremy Johnson," Candace said in a teasing voice, "did you just call me honey?" Suddenly her eyes widened in surprise. She realized that her mom was standing in her doorway!

"No, Candace," answered her mother, "I just wanted to tell you I'm off to my book club. I left a phone number on the fridge in case of an emergency. And, Candace, honey?"

"Yes, Mom?" asked Candace.

"I hope you're not planning on talking to that banana all afternoon," her mom said with a smile as she headed out the door.